I'M SO EMBARRASSED!

Robert Munsch

Illustrated by
Michael Martchenko

SCHOLASTIC CANADA LTD.
New York Toronto London Auckland Sydney
Mexico City New Delhi Hong Kong Buenos Aires

Scholastic Canada Ltd.
604 King Street West, Toronto, Ontario M5V 1E1, Canada

Scholastic Inc.
557 Broadway, New York, NY 10012, USA

Scholastic Australia Pty Limited
PO Box 579, Gosford, NSW 2250, Australia

Scholastic New Zealand Limited
Private Bag 94407, Greenmount, Auckland, New Zealand

Scholastic Children's Books
Euston House, 24 Eversholt Street,
London NW1 1DB, UK

The illustrations in this book were painted in watercolour on Crescent illustration board.
The type is set in Goudy Old Style MT 21 point.

Library and Archives Canada Cataloguing in Publication
Munsch, Robert N., 1945-

I'm so embarrassed! / Robert Munsch ; illustrated by
Michael Martchenko.

ISBN 0-439-95239-5

I. Martchenko, Michael II. Title.
PS8576.U575I58 2005a   jC813'.54   C2005-901037-1

ISBN-10 0-439-95239-5 / ISBN-13 978-0-439-95239-2

9 8 7 6   Printed in Canada   08 09

To Andrew Livingston and
Taylor Jae Gordon,
Cobalt, Ontario.
— R.M.

"**A**ndrew," said his mom, "let's go to the mall. You need some new shoes."

"NO!" said Andrew. "You always embarrass me when we go to the mall. You always say you are *not* going to embarrass me and you always *do*, so NO! I am not going to the mall."

"I promise not to embarrass you," said his mom.

"HA!" said Andrew, but he went anyway,
because he really needed to get new shoes.

Just at the door to the mall, Andrew's mother said, "Oh, Andrew! You didn't comb your hair."

So Andrew's mother spit on her hand and patted Andrew's hair till it was all flat.

"AHHHHH!" yelled Andrew. "*Spit!* Mommy-spit on my hair at the mall! *Very embarrassing!*"

"Oh, dear!" said Andrew's mom. "I am sorry about the spit. I keep forgetting how big you are. Don't worry. I will be very careful and will not embarrass you again."

"HA!" said Andrew.

So Andrew and his mom went walking down the mall, and Andrew saw his aunt.

"Please! Please!" said Andrew. "Don't say hello to my kissy aunt."

"Oh, Andrew," said his mom. "I have to say hello."

So Andrew's mom said hello, and Andrew's aunt gave him a big *hug*

SCRUNCH

and a large wet *kiss*

sPHLURt

that left lipstick all over his face.

"**GWACKHH!**" yelled Andrew. "Lipstick hugs and kisses! Lipstick hugs and kisses at the mall! I think I am going to die."

Andrew hid up in a tree.

Andrew's mom talked to his aunt for about three hours, and then she said, "Andrew? Where are you? Don't get lost. Why are you up in a tree?"

"I am definitely going to get lost if I don't stop getting hugs and kisses," said Andrew.

"Hugs are nice," said his mom.

"GWACKHH!" said Andrew.

They walked some more, and Andrew saw his teacher.

"Please," said Andrew. "Please, please, *please* do not let my mom say hi to my teacher."

But his mom yelled, *"Hello, Andrew's Teacher!* Andrew says you are his best teacher ever, and we are so happy that he got you for a teacher, and would you like to see some of Andrew's baby pictures?"

"AHHHHH!" yelled Andrew. "Baby pictures! AHHHHHH!"

"Andrew," said his mom, "stand beside your teacher. I am going to take a picture."

Andrew ran away. His mom found him and said, "Andrew, why are you hiding behind a trash can?"

"Baby pictures!" said Andrew. "You showed baby pictures to my teacher. Very embarrassing! You promised you were not going to embarrass me."

"OK! OK! OK!" said his mom. "I will be very careful and I will not embarrass you any more. I'm sorry. I'm sorry."

"Look," said Andrew. "There is Taylor-Jae from my school. How about I stay with Taylor-Jae, and you go shop by yourself for a while."

"Good idea," said Andrew's mom.

"Taylor-Jae," said Andrew, "I am going nuts. My mom is embarrassing me all over the place. I am glad you are here, so my mom will leave me alone."

"Maybe you should not be so glad," said Taylor-Jae. "Here comes *my* mom!"

Taylor-Jae's mom came up and said, "Taylor-Jae, do you want me to buy the pink underpants or the yellow underpants?"

"AHHHHHH!" yelled Taylor-Jae. "Underpants in a boy's face!"

Andrew and Taylor-Jae ran across the mall and jumped into a trash can.

After a while their moms came
by and knocked on the trash can.
"Andrew," said his mom, "why
are you in the trash can?"

"I am here because I am so embarrassed," said Andrew.
"Me too!" said Taylor-Jae.
"I don't believe it. Underpants in a boy's face!"

25

"Now, now!" said their moms. "You're just too sensitive. You should not let things bother you so much."

"OK," said Andrew and Taylor-Jae. "Then this won't bother you!"

They jumped out of the trash can, ran into the middle of the mall and yelled, "Our moms snore like grizzly bears and blame it on our dads!"

Both moms yelled, "AHHHHHH!" and jumped into the trash can.

Andrew and Taylor-Jae knocked on the trash can and their moms yelled, "How could you embarrass us so?"

"Well," said Andrew and Taylor-Jae, "WE HAD GOOD TEACHERS!"